THIS WALKER BOOK BELONGS TO:

WILL YOU COME ON WEDNESDAY?

How Shoqia's mother can see the school play when she never leaves the house is just one of the challenges facing the pupils of Jubilee Park School, many of whom are from Hindu or Moslem families. Rahilla wants to celebrate Ramadan by fasting, like a grown-up; Safina has to choose between upsetting her aunt or breaking the school's clothing rule; Shazia has to mother her seven unruly younger brothers for a day; while Changis and Najma's task is to find a "grandma" and "grandpa" to take their harvest festival food boxes!

WALKER STORYBOOKS

The Adventures of Rama and Sita
  by Ruskin Bond
Earthquake by Ruskin Bond
Hetty's First Fling by Diana Hendry
Our Horrible Friend by Hannah Cole
The Pepper Street Papers by Joan Smith
Robin Hood and Little John
  by Julian Atterton
Robin Hood and the Miller's Son
  by Julian Atterton
The Shape-Changer by Julian Atterton
Staples for Amos by Alison Morgan
We Three Kings from Pepper Street Prime
  by Joan Smith
The Wild Swans by Hans Christian Andersen
Will You Come on Wednesday?
  by Nadya Smith

Will you come on Wednesday?

First published 1987 by
Julia MacRae Books
This edition published 1990 by
Walker Books Ltd, 87 Vauxhall Walk
London SE11 5HJ

Reprinted 1990

Printed in Great Britain by
Richard Clay Ltd, Bungay, Suffolk

British Library Cataloguing in Publication Data
Smith, Nadya
Will you come on Wednesday?
I. Title
823'.914   PZ7
ISBN 0-7445-1462-2

Will you come on Wednesday?

Written by
NADYA SMITH

Illustrated by
BARBARA WALKER

WALKER BOOKS
LONDON

Contents

1 "Will you come on Wednesday?"

Every summer, the children at Shoqia's school did a play for their parents. There would be dressing up and singing, and some children would dance, and some children would play instruments. The mothers and fathers and small brothers and sisters, and grandmothers and grandfathers, and aunts and uncles would all come at half past nine in the morning.

They would watch the play, then they would have cups of tea or orange squash and a biscuit, and afterwards they would go into the classrooms and see the children's work and talk to the teachers. Everybody loved the Day of the Play.

This year the play was a very exciting one.

It was about seven princesses and a witch and a dragon. All the boys wanted to be the dragon because there was a lovely dragon costume with gold spikes all down the back, and a long, swishy tail, and claws to wear on their fingers –

but Mrs Davis chose Shamila because she was the right size for the costume, and she could move her arms and legs slowly, just like a dragon crawling along, and she had a nice, loud voice as well.

All the girls wanted to be a princess, so Mrs Davis made each one say some words from the play to see if she had a big voice, and do a little dance to see if she 'moved well'. She chose Shoqia to be Princess Ambreen. Then she chose three boys to be the prince, and the king, and an old man, and she chose a very tiny little boy called Azar to be the king's messenger – and he was very lucky because he had a shiny, yellow hat to wear and a silver trumpet to blow.

"Now I must choose a witch," said Mrs Davis, and she made all the children who weren't already in the play creep round the hall, making themselves into nasty, spiky

shapes. She chose Shazad. So now there were five boys in the play and eight girls, and some more children who played instruments.

The children practised and practised the play. Those who had things to say had their words written on pieces of card until they knew them so well that they didn't need the card any more. The princesses practised and practised their dance until it was quite perfect, and Prince Vishal and the dragon practised fighting. The bit that the children liked best was when the witch came flying down and chased all the princesses up the mountain with her broomstick. Sometimes the princesses seemed to be really frightened of the witch and started to scream, so that Mrs Davis had to tell Shazad not to be so scary.

All this time, the teachers and the ladies who helped them were cutting and fitting and sewing the costumes for the play. They made a fluffy, white beard for the king, and crowns for the king, the prince, and all the princesses. They made long dresses and cloaks and tunics, and, for the witch, a tall, black hat. At last, everything was ready. Mrs Davis made a big notice to go up outside the school. It said,

JUBILEE PARK SCHOOL

COME AND SEE OUR PLAY –

THE SEVEN PRINCESSES
AND THE DRAGON

ON FRIDAY AT 9.30

Tea and Biscuits afterwards.

On the Monday before the play, Mrs Davis said to the children, "Put your hand up if your mother or your father is coming to the play on Friday. We want to know how many chairs to put out, and how many cups of tea we'll have to make." Lots of children put their hands up, but Shoqia didn't.

"Is your mother coming, Shoqia?" asked Mrs Davis.

"No," said Shoqia. "My mummy stays at home."

"Perhaps your father could come then?" Mrs Davis said.

"No, my father's at work," said Shoqia.

11

"What a shame!" said Mrs Davis. "Don't you think your mother could come for just one hour on Friday – to see you in the play? I'm sure she would enjoy it."

Shoqia shook her head. "No," she said. "Mummy doesn't go out. She stays at home."

At dinner time, Mrs Davis said to Shoqia, "Does your mother stay at home all the time?"

"Yes," said Shoqia.

"Doesn't she ever want to go out?"

"No."

"What does she do all day?"

"She does sewing," said Shoqia. "She makes our clothes." She showed Mrs Davis her dress, all embroidered with beautiful flowers. "She

looks after my baby brothers and sisters, and does the cooking, and sometimes her friends come to see her."

"Well, I think your mother would like to see you in the play," said Mrs Davis. "I'm going to see what I can do."

Mrs Davis went to see the Headmistress and, that afternoon, she asked the lady who helped

in her classroom to write a letter to Shoqia's mother, in Urdu.

It said: *We would like to come and do our play for you in your house. May we come, please?* and she gave it to Shoqia to take home with her.

The next morning, Shoqia's father came to school. He said, "Thank you for your letter. My wife would like to see the play. Will you come on Wednesday, please?"

On Wednesday, the children in the play were very excited. In the morning, they practised their dancing and singing, and after dinner some big children from the Juniors came to help them get ready. Everybody put on their costumes, and Mrs Davis got the tape recorder with the dancing music, and the instrument children put their drums and tambourines and triangles into a big basket. At last they were ready to go!

Everybody stopped and stared as they came out into the road. First of all came Mrs Davis carrying the basket of instruments and the tape recorder. Then came Azar, the king's messenger, in his shiny yellow hat, going toot, toot on his silver trumpet. Behind him came the king and the prince wearing their golden crowns and splendid clothes, and behind them, the seven princesses in their beautiful long dresses and saris. They had lipstick on and pink stuff on their cheeks and eye shadow, and some of them had painted their nails pink

as well. Mrs Grant, the Headmistress, had said
that, just for today, they might wear dangly
ear-rings and bangles and sandals with heels.
Their hair was all braided with ribbons and
flowers. Behind them came the old man and
the witch, who pretended to ride on his broom,
and last of all there was the dragon, stomping
along, waving her claws in the air and looking
so fierce that the little children watching from
their garden gates ran indoors crying for their
mothers.

The procession went round the corner and
right up the road until it came to Shoqia's
house. Mrs Davis knocked on the door and,

after a while, the letter-box opened and two
little eyes peeped out.

"That's my little brother," said Shoqia, and

she shouted through the letter-box to tell him to get a chair and open the door.

They heard a chair being pulled along the passage, then the door opened and in they went.

Shoqia's mother was in the back room. She was very shy, and when she saw Mrs Davis, she pulled her *du'patta* across her face. But when the children came in wearing their lovely costumes, she smiled and laughed and clapped her hands.

A lot of friends and relations, many of them with small children, had come to watch the

play in Shoqia's house, and the room was very crowded. They pulled the sofa across one corner to make the king's palace, and they moved an armchair in front of the door to the kitchen to make the witch's cave. The audience sat on cushions at the other end of the room.

The play was about seven princesses who wanted to marry handsome Prince Vishal. The first one was very beautiful, the second one was rich, and the third one was clever.

The fourth one loved cooking, the fifth one loved picnics and parties, and the sixth one had a palace at the bottom of the sea. Princess

Ambreen was the seventh one. She was kind and gentle.

Prince Vishal loved them all. He could not make up his mind which one he wanted to marry, so he told them that he would choose his bride the next day.

The princesses were dancing in the palace garden, when along came an old witch who lived in a mountain cave nearby. She was looking for a wife for her dragon son, Gozo.

When the princesses saw her, they screamed with fright. They tried to run away, but the witch swept them up with her broom and chased them up the mountainside to her cave.

The prince came out to look for the princesses and found that they had gone. An old man,

who worked in the gardens, told him what had
happened. At once the prince jumped on his
horse and galloped to the rescue.

When he came to the dragon's cave there
was a terrible fight and the dragon ran away.

Prince Vishal was going to take the princesses
home, but the witch appeared and said that she
would kill them all if any one of them tried to
go.

Then Princess Ambreen came out and said
that she would marry the dragon if all the other
princesses were set free. The witch turned
round to see who was speaking and, in that
moment, Prince Vishal drew his sword and
struck her down.

Everybody was happy, and the prince

married Princess Ambreen because she was so kind and brave.

The play was a great success. The children remembered their words, and sang and danced and played their instruments better than ever before. From time to time, Shoqia stood up and told the mothers, in their own language, what the children in the play were saying.

The princesses had to do their dance again because the audience liked it so much, and when Prince Vishal fought the dragon, the small boys shouted with excitement.

When it was over, the children made a line across the room and bowed to the audience. The mothers clapped and clapped and shouted, "Very good!"

Mrs Davis said, "Thank you very much. We shall have to be getting back to school now."

But Shoqia said, "No, no! Mummy has made food for you. We can't go back to school till you have had the food!"

"Oh my goodness!" said Mrs Davis, looking at her watch. "We haven't got very much time – it's nearly the end of the afternoon."

"You must stay for the food," said Shoqia.
"It's all ready for you."

Shoqia's mother led the way into the front
room, and there was a table piled high with the
most delicious food! There were fried chicken
legs in a curry sauce, and *pecoras* and *samosas*,
and vegetables in different sauces, and bowls of
savoury rice and *chapattis* and *poppadoms*, and
fruit and biscuits and sweets and cakes.

"Please, please," said Shoqia's mother. "Sit."
She brought a chair for Mrs Davis. Then all
the children sat on the floor, and the mothers
handed round paper plates and everybody had
a wonderful feast.

"You're very kind," said Mrs Davis to

Shoqia's mother. "But you should not have gone to all that trouble!" But Shoqia's mother just smiled and smiled and put more food on Mrs Davis's plate.

Then Shoqia's father arrived. He had a camera, so everybody had to have their photograph taken.

Then it really was time to go.

"Thank you very much!" said Mrs Davis. "It's been a lovely afternoon!"

The children all said, "Thank you very much," too. Shoqia's mother took Mrs Davis's hand and said, "Thank you, thank you!" and smiled.

Then the children went back down the road to the school where their own mothers were waiting to take them home.

"Where have you been?" asked their mothers. "What have you been doing? What's it all about?"

But the children just said, "You must wait till Friday morning, and then it will be *your* turn!"

2 A long time to go

It was Ramadan, the month of the Fast. Every
day Rahilla asked her mother, "Is it Eid yet,
Mummy? Is it Eid today?"

Every day her mother said, "Not yet, Rahilla.
When the New Moon is seen in the sky, then it
will be Eid."

Eid-el-Fitr is the big celebration that Muslims
have at the end of the Fast. There are presents
and lovely food to eat. Everyone goes to the
Mosque to meet and pray together. Relations
come to the house and the children all get new
clothes and gifts of money. It is like some other
people's Christmas Day.

Every evening when it grew dark, Rahilla
would gaze out of the window at the sky,

23

looking for the new moon.

Her mother said, "You can't see it from this country, Rahilla. When they see the New Moon in Arabia, they will telephone to the big Mosque in London, and the people in the big Mosque will telephone to all the other Mosques in the country and they will tell us when it is Eid."

Rahilla did not like the month of the Fast. Every night after she had gone to sleep, she would be woken up by her mother and father and the big children getting up. They would wash and dress and say their prayers, then they would sit down to a big meal at two o'clock in the morning. They would talk and eat and be together.

Rahilla would lie in bed, listening to the talk.

She could smell the delicious smell of the food drifting up from downstairs and, although she was too sleepy to want any, she did not like to

be left out. Sometimes she would creep out of
bed and down the stairs to where the family
was eating and sometimes her mother would
let her stay and have something, and at other
times she would be cross and send her back to
bed. The meal that the family ate then was all
that they would have until nine o'clock the
next evening. It was a long time to go.

Rahilla was the youngest in the family. All

her brothers and sisters were allowed to fast like their parents.

"I want to fast. I want to fast," said Rahilla.

"You're too little," said her mother. "Wait until you're as big as Ali, then you can fast like the rest of us."

"No! I want to fast *now*! I want to fast *now*!" said Rahilla.

Then her mother got cross. She said, "You're too little. Now don't let me hear any more about it."

"Why do people fast then?" asked Rahilla.

"Because God has told us to. And also it helps us to remember all those people who never have enough to eat," said her mother. "People who are always hungry, and who sometimes die because they are so hungry."

In spite of what her mother had said, Rahilla decided that she was going to fast. She thought, I shall fast for a whole day, and then Mummy will see that I am as big as the others.

Rahilla's parents were always asleep in bed when she left for school. They were tired after being awake so long at night. Often, long after the meal had been cleared away and the children had gone back to bed, they would stay awake to pray and read the Koran.

Her big sister used to give her something to eat – cornflakes or bread and jam. This morning,

Rahilla hid the bread and jam under a chair before she left.

In school, at milk time, when the milk monitors were giving out the bottles, Rahilla said, "I don't want any today – and no biscuits either."

"Why don't you want your milk?" asked her

teacher, Mrs Davis. "Your mother has paid for it, you know – and for biscuits. She wants you to have them every day."

"I don't want any," said Rahilla, and shut her lips tightly.

Mrs Davis put the milk and biscuits down in front of Rahilla and said, "Come along now – try and have them, there's a good girl!"

Rahilla wanted to drink that milk. She wanted, more than anything, to eat the biscuits. But she knew that she had decided to fast, so she said, "I don't want it thank you," and she left them there until it was playtime, and Mrs Davis said, "Oh well, if you won't have it, you won't. But I shall send a note to your mother to let her know."

When it was dinner time, Rahilla tried to stay out in the playground, but the dinner lady collected up all the children, and when Rahilla said, "I don't want dinner today," the dinner lady said, "Nonsense! Go and wash your hands and get into the line."

Rahilla went into the dinner hall. She took a tray and went to the counter where the cooks

28

were serving out the dinners. They gave her
fish fingers, potato and carrots, and there was
sponge pudding and custard. Rahilla felt so
hungry she thought she would start to cry. She

took her tray to the table and she said, "I don't
want any thank you."

The dinner ladies came up to her. They tried
to make her eat. They put some fish and potato
on a fork and held it by her mouth saying,
"Come on lovey – just try it." But Rahilla
would not open her mouth. They fetched Mrs
Davis, who said, "She didn't have any milk

either today. I think the child must be ill."
And she felt Rahilla's forehead and sent her to
lie down in a special little room where sick
children went.

When it was time for afternoon school, Mrs
Davis came and asked Rahilla if she would like
to go home.

"No thank you," said Rahilla, "I'd like to go
back to the classroom."

That afternoon was Hobby Afternoon. The
children were allowed to choose what they
would like to do. Some of the children went

with the lady who helped Mrs Davis to make cakes in the school kitchen. They made fairy cakes with pink icing on top, and there were thirty six of them – one for each child and one for the teachers. "I don't want one thank you," Rahilla said, very near to tears. She could hardly stop herself from snatching up the little cake and stuffing it into her mouth.

"Oh come along – do eat one, Rahilla," said Mrs Davis.

Rahilla took a cake and gave it to Manjit who sat next to her, "Would you like it, Manjit?" she said.

"Oh yes please!" said Manjit. She ate the two cakes very quickly.

When Rahilla got home, her mother was in the bedroom sewing. Rahilla went to watch the television. Her tummy was really hurting. She knew that her mother did not start to prepare the evening meal until eight o'clock, when it was dark, and she herself was getting ready for bed. She waited and waited until at last her mother and grandmother went into the kitchen to start the cooking. Rahilla began to smell the

31

rich smells of curry and spices. She could hear
her grandmother rolling and slapping the
chapattis. She held her tummy and rocked
about. I don't like fasting, she thought, I'm glad
I don't have to do it every day.

When the meal was ready, Rahilla rushed
into the kitchen to fetch her plate. Her mother
gave her some rice and curry and *chapattis*.

"Can I have more?" asked Rahilla.

Her mother was surprised but she put some
more on the plate. Rahilla sat down on the floor
and ate it all up in just a few minutes.

32

"Why, Rahilla!" said her mother. "You look as if you haven't eaten for a week!" Rahilla hid her face in her hands.

"Have you had anything to eat today?" said her mother. Rahilla shook her head. She went to her coat and fetched the note from Mrs Davis.

"Why didn't you eat your dinner – and your milk and biscuits?" asked her mother when she had read it. "Are you sick?"

"I wanted to remember the little children who don't have enough to eat. I wanted to fast like the others," said Rahilla.

Her mother smiled. "Well, now you know what it feels like, do you still want to fast?"

"No," said Rahilla, munching a *chapatti*, "I don't like it at all. I think I'll wait till I'm bigger."

3 No bangles

Safina was on her way to school and she was very unhappy. The reason that she was unhappy was that the Headmistress had told the children that none of the girls must wear bangles, or sandals with high heels, or dangly ear-rings. She had said that one day a girl had fallen down in the playground, and her glass bangles had broken and cut her arm so badly that she had to go to hospital and have some stitches put in. She had said that one day a naughty boy had pulled a girl's ear-ring and made her ear bleed, and she had said that if you try to run about with high-heeled sandals on, you might fall and hurt yourself.

Now Safina had an aunt who had just come

back from Pakistan and brought her a beautiful
shalwar-kameez, made of pink silk, twelve

shining glass bangles, a pair of gold sandals
with high heels and some lovely dangly
ear-rings, all red and silver, and she had put
them on Safina. Safina's mother had to soap her

hands and arms to get the bangles on because they would only just go over her hands. When she was all dressed up, Safina looked beautiful; but then she remembered what Mrs Grant, the Headmistress, had said.

"Please, Mummy, take off my bangles and ear-rings, because I mustn't wear them at school," said Safina. But her mother could not understand.

"All girls wear bangles and ear-rings," she

said. "Look, even your baby cousin has bangles and ear-rings. I'm sure the teachers won't mind. Tell them that they're a present from Pakistan."

Safina tried to explain, but all her mother said was, "Your aunt will be very upset if you don't wear those lovely things. Now get your coat on and don't be late for school."

As Safina came round the corner, she saw her two friends, Rina and Michelle. They ran up to her, and when they saw the things that Safina's aunt had brought, they wanted to try them on. Rina wanted the sandals and Michelle wanted the ear-rings.

Then Rina said, "Ooh – you're going to get into trouble, Safina. You're not allowed to wear any of those things in school."

"I know," said Safina. She felt like crying. "I tried to tell Mummy but she didn't understand. What will the teachers say?"

"They'll tell you off," said Rina. "They'll make you stand out in front and show everybody."

"I know . . ." said Safina. "I'll take them off now and put them on again before I go home."

Rina took the ear-rings out. She had to undo a little gold fastening behind Safina's ears.

"What about the sandals?" said Michelle. "They're sure to notice those."

"I'll put my pumps on and leave these in my coat pockets," said Safina. Then she tried to take the bangles off, but they were very tight, and the more she pulled and pushed, the more difficult it became. Her hands began to swell up and they got so hot and sticky that she had to stop trying.

"Never mind," said Rina, "you can pull your

cardigan sleeves right down and nobody will see."

That morning, in Assembly, Safina sat very quietly. She did not whisper or fidget or do anything that would make anybody notice her, but at the end of Assembly Mrs Grant said, "I hope no one is wearing any bangles or ear-rings or high heels today."

She went all along the rows, looking at the children's feet and ears. Safina sat as quiet as a mouse. "Everybody put their arms up!" said Mrs Grant. "Touch the ceiling if you can!" She always said that.

Safina put her arms up very carefully and

just managed to hide the bangles with her cardigan sleeves.

"Very good, children," said Mrs Grant. "You may go to your classrooms."

In the classroom, Safina felt very unhappy.

39

She kept pulling at the sleeves of her cardigan until Mrs Davis, her teacher, said, "Is anything the matter, Safina? Are you too hot? Would you like to take your cardigan off?"

"No, I'm not hot – I'm not hot at all, thank you," said Safina hurriedly.

At dinner time, Rina and Safina ran to the cloakroom. They put soap on Safina's hands and tried to pull the bangles off, but they still would not come, and Safina had to go in to dinner with them on.

That afternoon it was P.E. Mrs Davis told the children to take everything off except their vests and knickers. Everybody got ready except Safina, who sat at her desk looking very unhappy.

"Is everybody ready?" called Mrs Davis. Then she saw Safina. "Why, what's the matter? Come on, you old slowcoach! We're all waiting for you!"

Safina said nothing, and then, as Mrs Davis came up to see what was wrong, she just started to cry.

"It's her bangles, Mrs Davis," said Rina.

"Her mummy put them on and she can't get them off, and she's scared she'll get into trouble."

"Dear me!" said Mrs Davis. She pulled off the cardigan and there were poor Safina's wrists and hands, all red and swollen. "Why didn't you tell me, Safina?" she said. "Nobody's going to be cross with you. Now

you get changed and come and do P.E. and
tonight I'll give you a letter for your mother to
explain to her why we don't like you to wear
bangles in school."

Safina cheered up at once. She did P.E. and
then she went out to play, and was very careful
not to fall over.

That afternoon, Mrs Davis asked a teacher
who could speak Punjabi, to write a letter to

Safina's mother, to explain about bangles and
ear-rings and sandals with heels.

When Safina's mother read the letter she
understood at once, and the next morning,
when Safina's hands were not swollen any
more, she put some soap on and slid the bangles
off quite easily.

"You can wear them in the holidays," she
said.

And Safina did.

4 "I'm Mother today!"

Shazia was nine years old. She lived with her father, who worked in a factory, her mother, who did sewing at home, and her seven younger brothers: Sajid, Majid, Rafiq, Zahir, Shiraz, Akmal and Arshad, who was only a baby. Shazia worked hard all day. When she was not at school or at Mosque school, she helped her mother with the shopping and the cooking and the washing. She helped to mend the boys' clothes and to look after Arshad when her mother was busy. The boys never did any work in the house. No one expected them to.

One day the postman brought a letter for her mother. It was from Aunt Yasmin in Bradford.

She wrote that she was ill in bed and wanted Mother to go and see her on Saturday. Usually, when Mother had to go on a visit, one of the aunts or grandmothers would come to stay, but they had all gone to Pakistan for a wedding and there was no one to help.

"Can you look after the boys till Sunday?" Mother asked Shazia.

"Yes," said Shazia.

So the next morning Father went off to the factory, and Mother went to get the coach to Bradford, leaving Shazia in charge.

The boys slept in two big beds upstairs. Because their mother was not there, they decided that they would not get up.

"You can't make us!" shouted Sajid, who was seven.

They all hid under the covers.

"Oh yes I can," said Shazia firmly, "I'm Mother today." She pulled and tugged the blankets off the beds, then smacked her brothers until they were hopping about on the floor, (except for the baby, Arshad, who was still asleep).

45

"Now get dressed," she said.

"We won't!" said the boys.

"Then I shall dress you – like babies," said Shazia.

But she had forgotten which clothes belonged to each boy. She tried to put Akmal's little pants on Majid, who was six, and she put Majid's big jumper on little Shiraz, who was only three. She put one of Arshad's tiny socks on Rafiq, who was five, and Sajid's long trousers on Akmal – how he screamed! The

trousers came right up over his head. They did look a funny lot. It took Shazia a long time to sort them out.

"That's done then," she said at last. "Now you must wash."

"We won't! We won't!" shouted those naughty boys.

"Very well. Then I will wash you – like babies," said Shazia.

She fetched a wet cloth and wiped their hands and faces, then she put oil on their heads

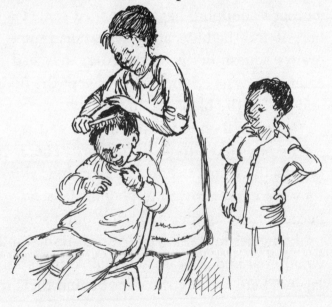

and brushed their hair till it shone.

"Now we must eat," she said. "What do you all want?"

"Chips," said Sajid

"Chocolate," said Majid.

"*Pecoras*," said Rafiq.

"Ice lolly," said Zahir.

"Sweets," said Shiraz and Akmal together.

"O'nj! O'nj!" shouted Arshad.

Shazia found some cornflakes and milk in the kitchen cupboard and some crisps in her mother's shopping bag. She boiled some tea for herself and the boys and gave Arshad some orange squash in his bottle. After they had eaten, she washed the dishes, swept the floors and folded the blankets on the beds.

"Now we'll go to the park," she said.

The boys liked to go to the park. There were swings there and a slide and a sandpit, although they were not allowed to play in the sand because their mother had once found some broken glass in it. Shazia dressed Arshad in his woolly hat and anorak, and tied Akmal's shoe laces. Then, locking the door behind them, the children went out into the street. They went first to the corner shop which was kept by Ishfaq Hussain and his wife, Coser. Shazia bought some bubble gum, and Coser gave them an apple each and a big bag of broken biscuits to eat in the park.

They crossed the road at the Pelican crossing, waiting until they saw the green man light up, and very soon they came to the park. They played on the swings and the slide, they fed the pigeons, and Sajid and Majid had a sand fight,

although Shazia said they were not to. Then they lay on the grass and ate the apples and biscuits until it was time to go home.

It was getting dark by the time they reached the front door. As soon as they got inside, Sajid ran to switch on the television. He wanted to watch the football. Rafiq switched over to the cartoons. Sajid switched it back. They began to fight.

"Oh, stop it, you two!" shouted Shazia who was tired after carrying Arshad on her back. She went out to the kitchen to fetch the rice and *pecoras* which her mother had left ready for their tea. When she came back, the boys were watching the football. Rafiq was crying. Shazia

handed out the bowls, then she said, "Where's Akmal?"

They looked round the room. Akmal was not there. He was not in the front room which was always kept closed for visitors; he was not in the kitchen or in the backyard.

"We must have left him in the park," said Majid.

Shazia began to cry. "We've lost Akmal!" she sobbed. "What will Mummy say?"

Just then she heard her father's key in the door and she rushed to him, crying, "Akmal's lost! We left him in the park! What can we do, Daddy? What will Mummy say?"

Her father looked very worried but he said, "Don't cry Shazia; you stay here with the little ones, and Sajid and Majid can come to the park with me."

"But we're watching the match!" wailed Sajid.

"No you're not," said his father, switching off the set. "Go and get your coats – quickly now."

After they had gone, Shazia went to the

kitchen. She looked in all the cupboards. She looked in the oven. She opened the door to the

cellar and called, "Akmal! Akmal". She did not want to go down those cold, dark steps by herself. She searched the cupboard under the stairs, where the children liked to hide and have secret tea parties.

Then she went out into the street and wandered about, calling to Akmal. Far away, she could hear the sound of an ambulance. Had Akmal run into the road and been knocked

down? Perhaps someone had taken him away –
her mother had told them never to talk to
strangers, but Akmal wouldn't understand that.
Soon her father and the boys came back.
They had not found Akmal.

"I shall have to go to the police," said her
father. "You'd better put the baby to bed,
Shazia. I'll be back as soon as I can."

Shazia went slowly upstairs with Arshad in
her arms. She kept thinking about poor little
Akmal alone in the dark. She switched on the
bedroom light, then gave a shriek, "Daddy!
Everyone! Come and see!"

Her father came running. There, in a corner
on a pile of washing, lay Akmal, fast asleep.

He had climbed the stairs by himself and made
a cosy nest in the clothes.

The next day, when her mother came home, Shazia was smiling.

"Were the boys good?" asked her mother.

"Not very – but I was," said Shazia.

"I'm glad to hear that," said her mother, "because Aunt Yasmin has sent you a present."

It was a beautiful red and gold necklace. Shazia put it on at once, and looked in the mirror.

"Your aunt is better now," said her mother. "I shan't have to go back again."

Shazia was pleased about that. For as she told of all the trouble her naughty brothers had given her, and the fright she had had when she thought Akmal was lost, she felt that being mother for one day was enough for quite some time to come.

5 A present for Harvest

Everybody thought that Mr Goss's classroom looked like a greengrocer's shop. This was because it was harvest time and the children were bringing fruit and vegetables for their harvest festival. Mr Goss said that everyone must bring something, even if it was only one potato or one carrot, but most of the children brought more than that. Paul brought a bag of apples, Yasmin brought some tomatoes, and Razwan brought a big bag of grapes from his father's shop.

Mr Goss said that after the harvest assembly, all the food would be put into boxes, and taken round to the old people who lived near the school. He told the children that if they knew

of any grandmas or grandpas who lived alone
and would like a box of food, they should tell
him and he would put that old person's name
on his list.

Most of the children were puzzled. All their
grandmas and grandpas lived with their own
families. Mr Goss said that they were lucky –
but he knew of a lot of old people who didn't
have a family to look after them.

"Many of them," he said, "don't have enough
money to buy food or to keep themselves
warm."

On the morning of the harvest assembly, all
the fruit and vegetables and jars of jam and

tins of baked beans were arranged on tables at
one end of the hall. The school cook had made
a big piece of bread in the shape of a bundle of
wheat, and in among the stalks of the wheat
were lots of little bread mice, all shiny and
golden. Mr Goss said they were harvest mice.

Some of the smallest children had baskets
with apples and bananas and oranges in them,
and they came out to the front while the others
were singing their harvest song, and held their
baskets up so that everyone could see. Then
Mrs Grant told them about children all over the
world who didn't have enough to eat, and
about what everyone could do to try and help

them. She said that after dinner, when all the food had been sorted out and put into boxes, a few teachers and some of the children would take them round to the old people.

When they got back to their classroom, Mr Goss noticed the children whispering in a corner.

"What's the matter?" he asked.

No one wanted to say, but then Parveen said, "Changis and Najma saw two deaders when they were coming to school!"

Everyone stopped what they were doing and stared at Changis and Najma.

"What do you mean?" asked Mr Goss. "Do you mean that someone is dead?"

"Yes – two deaders. We saw them," said Changis.

Mr Goss went and sat at his desk. "Come over here, you two, and tell me what you saw. Was it a car accident? Was somebody knocked down in the road?"

Najma shook her head. "No," she said, "they're in a house."

Mr Goss didn't know what to think. "If

they're in a house," he said, "I think perhaps they were asleep."

"No," said Changis. "We shouted and they didn't move. And a big boy threw a stone."

Mr Goss decided that he would go and have a look. "But if you are making all this up," he told the children, "I shall be very, very angry."

Mr Goss found someone to look after his class, then he and Changis and Najma set off up the road. The children lived next door to each other in a road near the park, and always went to and from school together. Some of the houses in the streets nearby were going to be pulled down to make room for some new flats, and there were planks nailed across the doors and windows. The little front gardens were full of

tall weeds and thistles, and there was rubbish everywhere.

"That's the house!" cried Changis suddenly, pointing. "The one near the tree."

As they came up to the house, Mr Goss said, "But it's all boarded up – how could you see anything inside?" And then he understood.

Behind the straggly privet hedge in the front garden was an old mattress that somebody had thrown out. And on the mattress lay a very old man and a very old lady. They were fast asleep – Mr Goss could see them breathing – and they had piled all their things on top of them to keep themselves warm, newspapers, old coats and

shoes, boxes and boots and carrier bags, and a big old quilt which must have been thrown out with the mattress.

"They're not dead!" said Mr Goss. "They're asleep. Look at them breathing."

"They were dead when we saw them," said Changis.

As he spoke, there was a movement at the bottom of the pile. The old man opened his eyes and tried to sit up. He looked very angry and the children ran and hid behind Mr Goss.

For a long while the old man stared at Mr Goss, screwing up his little red eyes against the sunlight. Then he said in a scratchy voice, "You got a fag?"

"Er – I'm afraid not. I don't smoke. But – " Mr Goss felt in his pocket and brought out two £1 coins. "Here – get yourselves something to eat – there's a café just down the road."

The old man got to his feet and took the money. He didn't say "Thank you". He just nodded to Mr Goss, and shook the old lady, who woke up and began to complain. Together they started to collect their things, stuffing the papers and shoes into carrier bags, wrapping themselves in the coats.

Suddenly Najma said, "You're a grandma and a grandpa – you can have a box of food! We'll bring it after dinner."

"I don't think they'll be here after dinner, Najma," said Mr Goss, "I think they're getting ready to go."

"But they'll come back after dinner," said Najma, "and you said if we knew about a grandma and a grandpa who wanted a box of food . . ."

"Very well," said Mr Goss. "You're quite right, Najma. We'll come back after dinner."

When they got back to school, Changis and Najma helped to fill a box for the old man and

the old lady. Mr Goss said that it would be best to give them things that did not need to be cooked, because he thought that perhaps the grandma might not have a stove to cook on. So the children put in apples and grapes and biscuits, a packet of margarine and a jar of jam, and, for a treat, two of the cook's shiny bread mice.

"It's for our own grandma and grandpa," Najma said.

After dinner, the children went back to the house with Mr Goss. There was no sign of the

two old people. Everything had gone except the mattress.

"They might come back tonight," said Changis. He looked very sad. "Can we leave the box for them?"

They put the box under a corner of the mattress, so that even if it rained it would not get wet, and went back to school.

The next morning the two children came running into the classroom.

"They came back! They came back!" they told Mr Goss.

"How do you know?" asked Mr Goss. "Did you see them?"

"No – but all the things have gone – the box is empty! Do you think they were happy to have the food?"

"I hope they were," said Mr Goss. "I hope they had a very happy harvest."

Until recently, Nadya Smith was a teacher at a multicultural school in Birmingham, very similar to the one in this book. She has now written a second title about the pupils of Jubilee Park, called *Imran's Secret* (published as a Julia MacRae Redwing, 1990). She has three grown-up children.

Here are some more WALKER STORYBOOK titles for you to enjoy

The Adventures
of
Rama and Sita

by Ruskin Bond

(black and white illustrations
by Valerie Littlewood)

When Prince
Rama and
his beloved Sita
are forced into exile
in the dangerous Forest
of Dandak, they find themselves
up against the powerful and evil Ravana,
King of the Demons,
and in the middle
of a very exciting
and dramatic series
of adventures.

A WALKER STORYBOOK

Our Horrible Friend

by Hannah Cole

(black and white illustrations by Julie Stiles)

Like Diane and Jenny, Poppy lives with her mum and visits her dad on Saturdays.

But when Poppy and her mum start visiting Diane and Jenny's dad on Saturdays, the two sisters are not at all pleased. And this is just the first of several surprises...

A WALKER STORYBOOK

ROBIN HOOD
and *LITTLE JOHN*

by Julian Atterton

(black and white illustrations by
John Dillow)

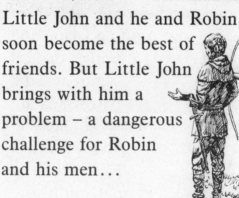

One day, when walking
in the forest, Robin
Hood encounters a
huge stranger – and
ends up in the river!
The man is, of course,
Little John and he and Robin
soon become the best of
friends. But Little John
brings with him a
problem – a dangerous
challenge for Robin
and his men…

A WALKER STORYBOOK

STAPLES
FOR
AMOS

by Alison Morgan
(black and white illustrations
by Charles Front)

When Mum forgets to
buy staples for Amos
to mend the fence of the
bullock field, Daley acts quickly to try
and save her from the
anger of the old farm
worker. But his action
leads him into danger...

"A story of courage and determination...
A simple, imaginative and rather
moving tale."
British Book News

A WALKER STORYBOOK

EARTHQUAKE

by Ruskin Bond

(black and white illustrations by
Valerie Littlewood)

"What do you do when there's
an earthquake?" asks Rakesh.
Everyone in the Burman
household has their own
ideas, but when the tremors
begin and everything starts to shake and
quake, to crack and
crumble, they are
taken by surprise...

A WALKER STORYBOOK

The Pepper Street Papers

by Joan Smith

(black and white illustrations
by Nicole Goodwin)

When the Head announces
that Pepper Street Primary
may have to close, Sam
and his class decide
to commit the school to
floppy disc. Meanwhile,
Sam's sister Em appoints
herself official school
photographer. The result,
as ever, is chaos!

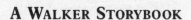

A WALKER STORYBOOK

^{The}Shape-Changer
by Julian Atterton
(black and white illustrations
by Nigel Murray)

When Kari, the son of a
Viking settler, comes to the
farmstead of Ellen and her
father, he discovers that a
terrible spell has been cast on them. He
promises to try and break
it – but can a mere
boy really overcome
such powerful and frightening magic?

"A superbly crafted story."
British Book News

A WALKER STORYBOOK

Hetty's First Fling

by Diana Hendry
(black and white illustrations by
Nicole Goodwin)

Great Uncle Fergus's
seventy-fifth
birthday party
means a trip
to the Isle of Skye for the Mungoe family –
and, for Hetty in particular, a very special
knees up indeed!

A WALKER STORYBOOK

MORE WALKER PAPERBACKS
For You to Enjoy